Dec. 5, 2016

Happy 2nd birthday, L

We hope you enjoy thi

Love,

Auntie Jenice and

Uncle Glen

D0607254

This edition published by Parragon Books Ltd in 2016 and distributed by

Parragon Inc.
440 Park Avenue South, 13th Floor
New York, NY 10016
www.parragon.com

Copyright © Parragon Books Ltd 2012–2016
Text © Hollins University

All rights reserved. No part of this publication may be reproduced, stored in a retrieval system or transmitted, in any form or by any means, electronic, mechanical, photocopying, recording or otherwise, without the prior permission of the copyright holder.

ISBN 978-1-4748-3278-6

Printed in China

# Count to 10 with a mouse

Parragon

Bath • New York • Cologne • Melbourne • Delhi
Hong Kong • Shenzhen • Singapore • Amsterdam

There was a little mouse

no bigger

than a

mole,

who lived in a round place

that he called a hole.

He tried to count his nose,

he tried to count his toes.

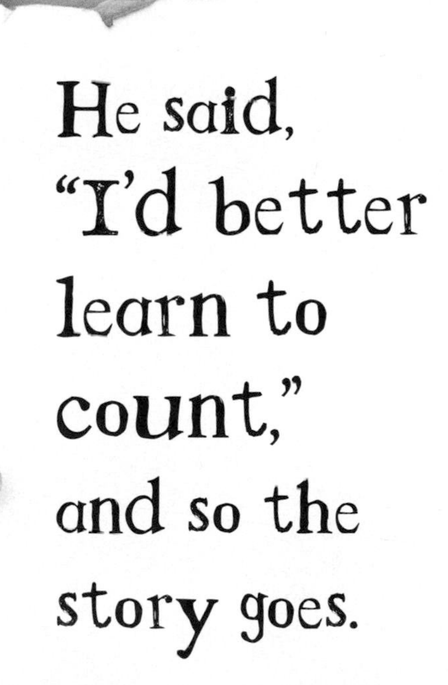

He said, "I'd better learn to count," and so the story goes.

## 1 mouse

One mouse, took one

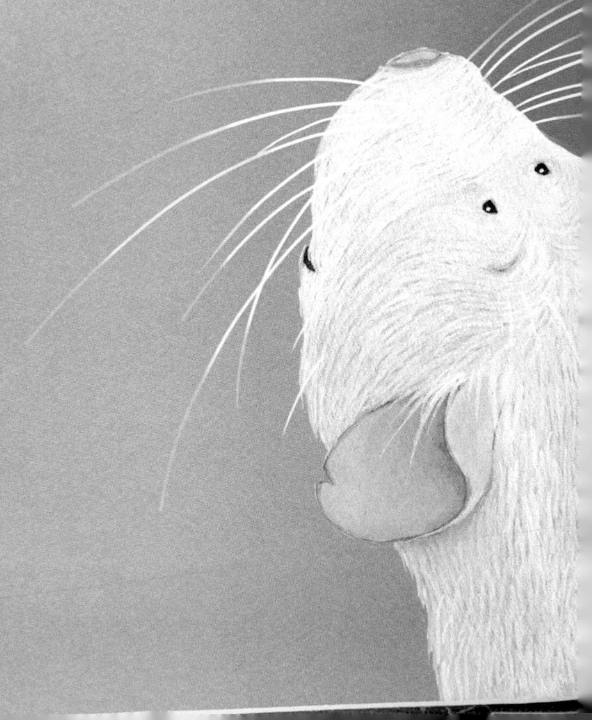

look,

at one book,

that had one hole
to run through.

# 2 holes

Then the mouse ran through the book,

the mouse ran through the book.

He ran onto the next page

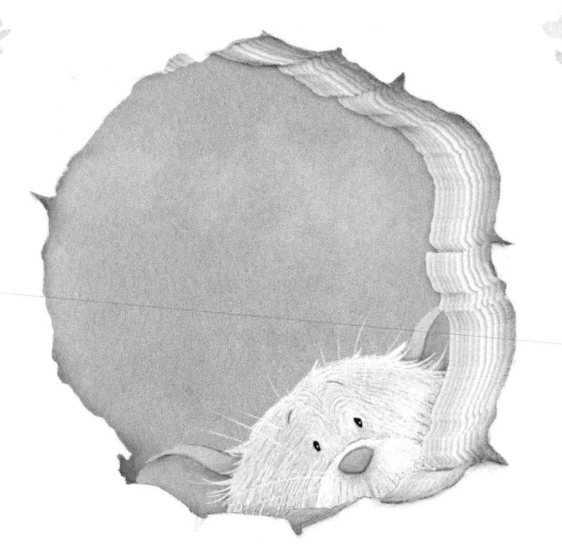

to take a little look.

# 3 fish

And there, what does he see?
And there, what does he see?

Three little fishes

# Swimming in the sea.

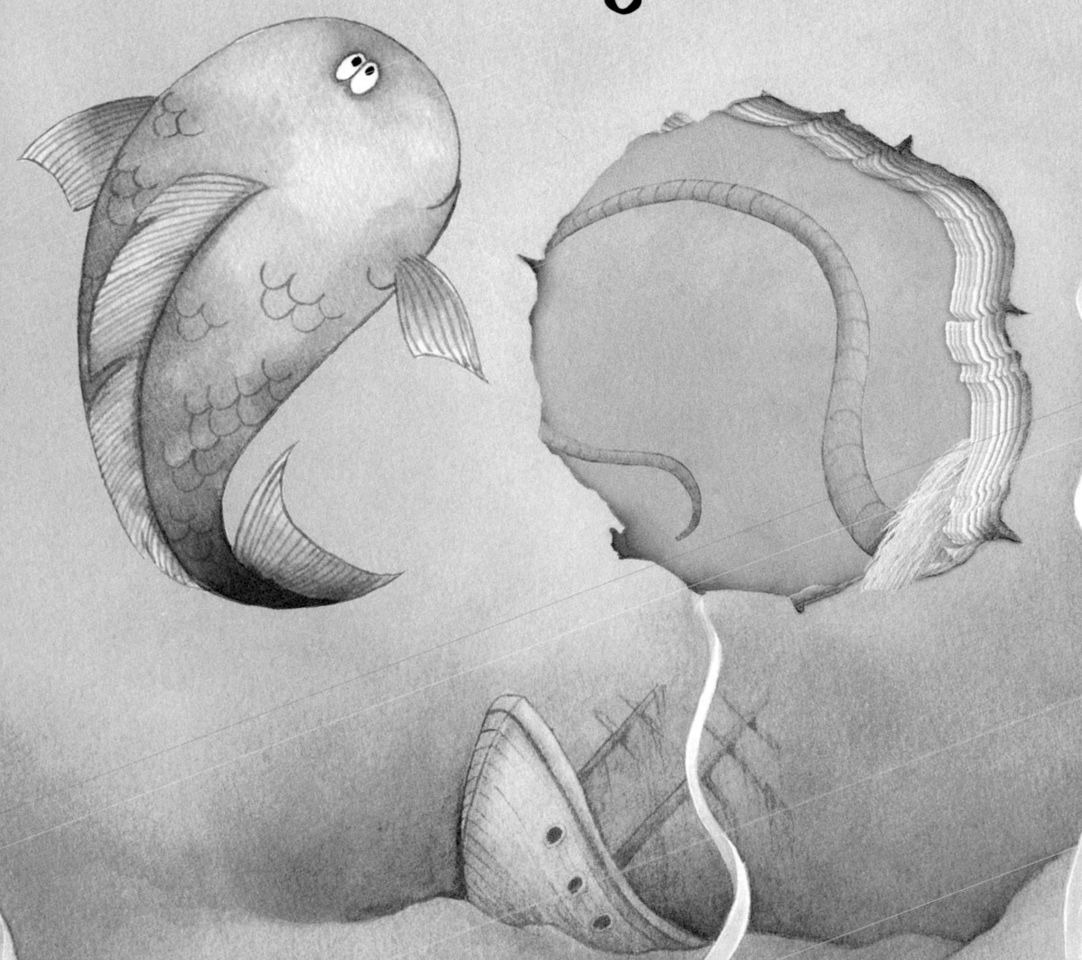

Then the mouse ran through the book,
the mouse ran through the book.
He ran onto the next page
to take a little look.

# 4 monkeys

And there, what does he see?
And there, what does he see?

Four little monkeys

Swinging in a tree.

Then the mouse ran through the book,
the mouse ran through the book.
He ran onto the next page
to take a little look.

# 5 butterflies

And here, great sakes alive!
And here, great sakes alive!

Here he found five butterflies,
one, two, three, four, five.

Then the mouse ran through the book,
the mouse ran through the book.
He ran onto the next page
to take a little look.

# 6 pussycats

And in among the mix.
And in among the mix.

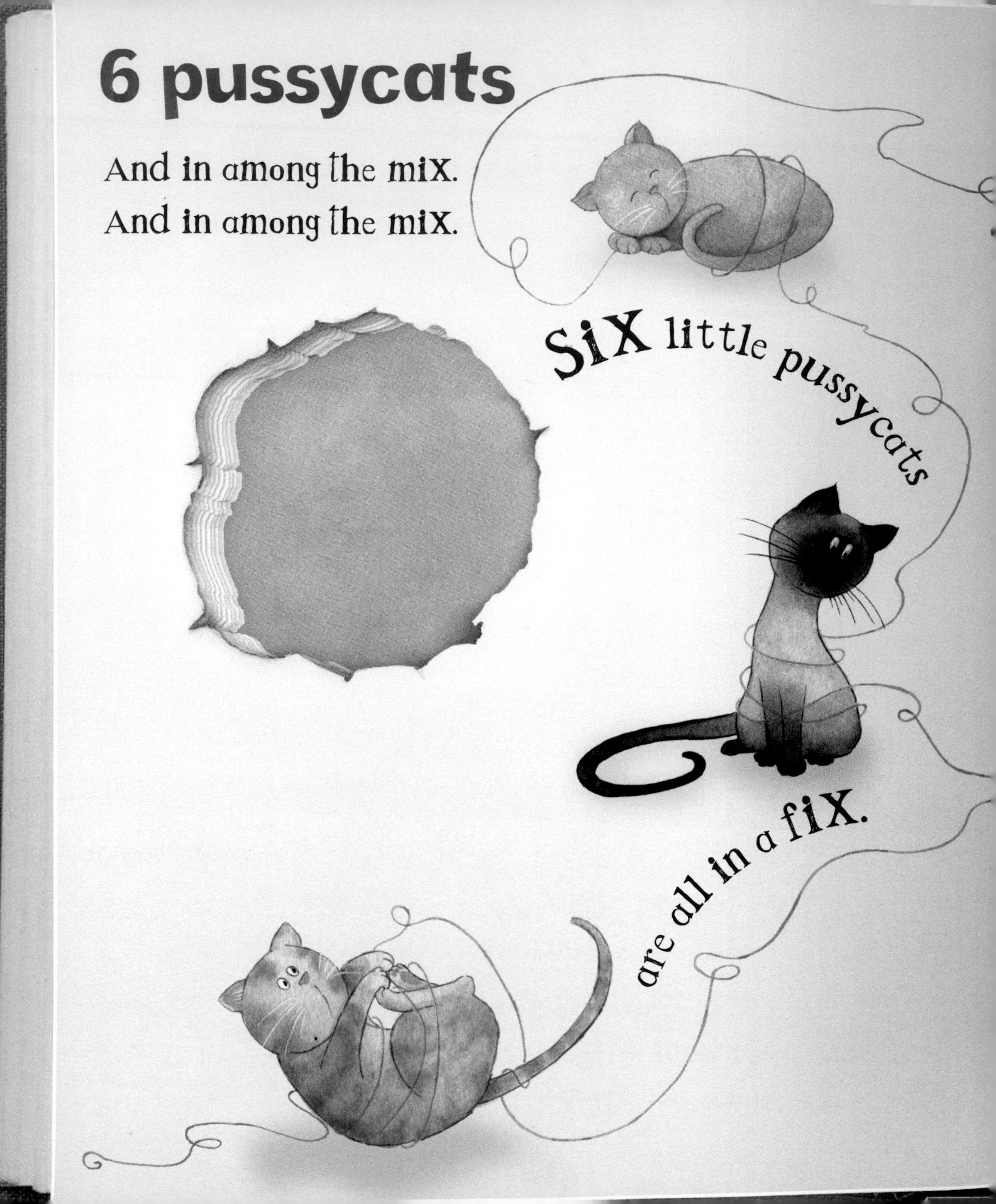

Six little pussycats are all in a fix.

So the mouse ran through the book,
the mouse ran through the book.
He ran onto the next page
to take a little look.

# 7 apples

And there, what does he see?
And there, what does he see?

upon an apple tree.

Then the mouse ran through the book,
the mouse ran through the book.
He ran onto the next page
to take a little look.

# 8 crows

And here is what he saw.
And here is what he saw.

caw!

Eight shiny black crows

Then the mouse ran through the book,
the mouse ran through the book.
He ran onto the next page
to take a little look.

# 9 o'clock

Here everything is fine,
the clock has just struck nine.
Nine o'clock is nine o'clock
and everything is fine.

Then Dockery Hickory Dock,
the Mouse ran **down** the clock.

Then the mouse ran through the book,
the mouse ran through the book.
He ran onto the next page
to take a little look.

1 2 3 4 5

And when he got to ten.

And when he got to ten.

6 7 8 9 10

He turned

around

the other way

and ran **right back** again.